D0463470

YOU'RE THE TOP

YOU'RE

THE TOP

A Love Song by Cole Porter

INTRODUCTION BY BOBBY SHORT

EDITED BY PAMELA PRINCE AND JANE HANDEL
DESIGN BY TIKA BUCHANAN, ERIC BAKER DESIGN ASSOCIATES
PHOTOGRAPHY BY KATRIN THOMAS

SIMON & SCHUSTER EDITIONS

INTRODUCTION

As any Broadway buff would certainly know, Cole Porter wrote his blockbuster tune "You're the Top" for the 1934 hit show, *Anything Goes*. Of the dozen or so songs completed for the show, five became standards and are still being recorded and performed regularly even today. But the zinger was "You're the Top," one of the first of a string of laundry-list songs Porter was to become famous for, a kind of trademark he would yield to time and time again in subsequent shows but never with the success of the somersaulting, leapfrogging rhymes and patterns he introduced for "You're the Top," with Porter's words artfully alternating between the sublime and the ridiculous but never quite descending to the banal.

When *Anything Goes* traveled to London in 1935, Porter refashioned the topical "You're the Top" to better suit the English audiences and many patently American references were removed to make way for subjects British theatergoers could easily recognize. The theater music historian Stanley Green has pointed out that a dress for Saks became a dress by Patou, and Bendel bonnet was suddenly an Ascot bonnet. Little digs were taken at Parliament; the royal family was spared.

In light of the drivel one is subjected to these days where most popular music is concerned, it seems all but impossible for such sophisticated fare to have enjoyed such widespread popularity only a few decades ago. But the images and the characters the worldly Porter placed before the English-speaking public proved all but irresistible back then and spread his wit and humor far and wide and from the lowly to, of course, the upper classes. This landslide of popular appeal invariably led to countless efforts on the part of his colleagues in the music business to imitate the Porter style, but Mr. and Mrs. America got into the act as well. Parodies of the song flourished quite openly, causing Porter to seek legal means to prevent them. According to one

Porter biographer, George Eels, he was so successful in doing so that, arriving at a broadcasting studio one day where he was scheduled to deliver yet another chorus, he was informed that he could not, due to the ban he himself had levied.

If "Night and Day" is Cole Porter's most celebrated song, then "You're the Top" certainly runs a very close second. Modern jazz musicians have always responded excitedly to the tricky and intriguing rhythms Porter composed though I've never cottoned to the updating some performers employ. What the almighty Cole put down in his song was a glittering chronicle of the uncertainty, the glamour and the dash of those between-the-wars years in America.

When I'm asked to sing "You're the Top," I have to stop and think lest I forget and plunge into some of the lines from that famous parody created by, they say, a close friend of Porter's shortly after the song was initially successful: "You're the breasts of Venus, you're King Kong's penis, you're self-abuse!" Kid stuff. Nevertheless, I often find myself bemused when I consider to what lengths some fin de siècle wag would travel should he decide to 'modernize' the Porter classic. Or better still, what would Porter be up to as we approach the twenty-first century? The theater being played out in the worlds of politics, society, art—and don't forget medical science—would provide him with a bonanza. Maybe it's just as well that he stopped when he was ahead.

Bobby Short

YOU'RE

THE TOP

YOU'RE

THE COLOSSEUM

YOU'RE THE TOP

YOU'RE THE LOUVRE MUSEUM

YOU'RE
A

A MELODY FROM SYMPHONY BY STRAUSS

YOU'RE A BENDEL

BONNET

A SHAKESPEARE SONNET

YOU'RE MICKEY MOUSE

U’RE
HE
LE

YOU'RE THE TOW'R OF PISA

YOU'RE THE SMILE ON THE MONA LISA

I'M

A WORTHLESS CHECK

A

TOTAL WRECK, A FLOP

BUT IF BABY I'M THE BOTTOM

YOU’RE

THE TOP

YOU'RE THE TOP

YOU'RE MAHATMA GANDHI

YOU'RE THE TOP

YOU'RE NAPOLEON

BRANDY

YOU'RE THE PURPLE LIGHT OF A SUMMER NIGHT IN SPAIN

YOU'RE THE NATIONAL GALL'RY

YOU'RE GARBO'S SAL'RY

YOU'RE

CELLOPHANE

YOU'RE SUBLIME

YOU'RE A TURKEY

DINNER

YOU'RE THE TIME OF THE DERBY WINNER

I'M A TOY BALLOON

THAT

IS FATED SOON TO POP

BUT IF BABY I'M THE BOTTOM

YOU'RE

THE TOP

Verse 1

At words poetic, I'm so pathetic
That I always have found it best,
Instead of getting 'em off my chest,
To let 'em rest unexpressed.
I hate parading
My serenading,
As I'll probably miss a bar,
But if this ditty
Is not so pretty,
At least it'll tell you
How great you are.

Refrain 1

You're the top!
You're the Colosseum.
You're the top!
You're the Louvre Museum.
You're a melody
from a symphony by Strauss,
You're a Bendel Bonnet,
A Shakespeare sonnet,
You're Mickey Mouse.
You're the Nile,
You're the Tow'r of Pisa,
You're the smile
On the Mona Lisa;
I'm a worthless check,
a total wreck, a flop,
But if, baby, I'm the bottom,
You're the top!

Verse 2

Your words poetic are not pathetic.
On the other hand, boy, you shine,
And I can feel after every line
A thrill divine
Down my spine.
Now gifted humans like Vincent Youmans
Might think that your song is bad,
But for a person who's just rehearsin'
Well, I gotta say this my lad:

Refrain 2

You're the top!
You're Mahatma Gandhi.
You're the top!
You're Napoleon brandy.
You're the purple light
of a summer night in Spain,
You're the National Gall'ry,
You're Garbo's sal'ry,
You're cellophane.
You're sublime,
You're a turkey dinner,
You're the time
Of the Derby winner.
I'm a toy balloon
that is fated soon to pop,
But if, baby, I'm the bottom,
You're the top!

Refrain 3

You're the top!
You're a Ritz hot toddy.
You're the top!
You're a Brewster body.
You're the boats that glide
on the sleepy Zuider Zee,
You're a Nathan panning,
You're Bishop Manning,
You're broccoli.
You're a prize,
You're a night at Coney,
You're the eyes
Of Irene Bordoni.
I'm a broken doll,
a fol-der-rol, a blop,
But if, baby, I'm the bottom,
You're the top!

Refrain 4

You're the top!
You're an Arrow collar.
You're the top!
You're a Coolidge dollar.
You're the nimble tread
of the feet of Fred Astaire,
You're an O'Neill drama,
You're Whistler's mama,
You're Camembert.
You're a rose,
You're Inferno's Dante,
You're the nose
On the great Durante.
I'm just in the way,
as the French would say "de trop,"
But, if baby, I'm the bottom,
You're the top!

Refrain 5

You're the top!
You're a Waldorf salad.
You're the top!
You're a Berlin ballad.
You're a baby grand
of a lady and a gent,
You're an old Dutch master,
You're Mrs. Astor,
You're Pepsodent.
You're romance,
You're the steppes of Russia,
You're the pants on a Roxy usher.
I'm a lazy lout
that's just about to stop,
But if, baby, I'm the bottom,
You're the top!

Refrain 6

You're the top!
You're a dance in Bali.
You're the top!
You're a hot tamale.
You're an angel, you,
simply too, too, too diveen,
You're a Botticelli,
You're Keats,
You're Shelley,
You're Ovaltine.
You're a boon,
You're the dam at Boulder,
You're the moon over Mae West's shoulder.
I'm a nominee
of the G.O.P., or GOP,
But if, baby, I'm the bottom,
You're the top!

Refrain 7

You're the top!
You're the Tower of Babel.
You're the top!
You're the Whitney stable.
By the river Rhine,
you're a sturdy stein of beer,
You're a dress from Saks's,
You're next year's taxes,
You're stratosphere.
You're my thoist,
You're a Drumstick Lipstick,
You're da foist
In da Irish Svipstick.
I'm a frightened frog
that can find no log to hop,
But if, baby, I'm the bottom,
You're the top!

Finale, Act 1

You're the top!
You're my Swanee River.
You're the top!
You're a goose's liver.
You're the boy who dares
Challenge Mrs. Baer's son, Max.
You're a Russian ballet,
You're Rudy Vallee,
You're Phenolax!!!!
You're much more,
You're a field of clover–
I'm the floor
When the ball is over.

Parody Version

You're the top!
You're Miss Pinkham's tonic.
You're the top!
You're a high colonic.
You're the burning heat
of a bridal suite in use,
You're the breasts of Venus,
You're King Kong's penis,
You're self-abuse.
You're an arch
In the Rome collection.
You're the starch
In a groom's erection.
I'm a eunuch who
has just been through an op.
But if, baby, I'm the bottom,
You're the top!

We would like to thank the following for their enthusiasm and generosity during the making of this book :

RAMONA BAJEMA - *model*
LENA BAKER - *model*
BONNIE BAKER - *muse and mother*
SADIE BIRDFEATHER - *technical assistant*
DAVID BLANKENSHIP - *model*
CAFE DES ARTISTES - *location*
CARTIER - *location*
KELLY CHRISTY - *milliner*
SUSAN ENOCHS - *model*
JANIS DONNAUD - *agent and...*
JANICE EASTON - *editor*
FLEA THE DOG - *model*
AMI GOODHEART - *model*
MENACHEM HAIMOVICH - *loyal landlord*
KAROLINA HENKE - *photo assistant*
KOKIN - *milliner*
GEORGE LANG - *of Cafe des Artistes*
ALESSANDRO MAGANIA - *model and dancer*
NICK McGLIBERY - *enthusiastic supporter*
RICHARD MERKIN - *model and friend*
EMIL MICCA - *of Sotheby's*
DEBBIE MOUNSEY - *mother*
JULIA MOUNSEY - *model*
TAKAYO MUROGA - *design assistant*
SANDRA MYHRBERG - *photo assistant*
HANS NEUBERT - *honest opinions*
MILA RADULOVIC - *model*
DAVID ROSENTHAL - *publisher*
SABISHA - *model and dancer*
BOBBY SHORT - *introduction and inspiration*
SOTHEBY'S - *location*
ANDREW STERN - *photo assistant*
KATRIN THOMAS - *photographer extraordinaire*
EVELYN VON GIZYCKI - *stylist*
JOAN WELSCH - *model*
CHRISTINA WYETH - *assistant to Bobby Short*

Gratefully, Eric Baker, Tika Buchanan, Jane Handel, and Pamela Prince

SIMON & SCHUSTER EDITIONS
ROCKEFELLER CENTER, 1230 AVENUE OF THE AMERICAS
NEW YORK, NEW YORK 10020

MANUFACTURED IN CANADA

1 3 5 7 9 10 8 6 4 2

LIBRARY OF CONGRESS CATALOGING IN PUBLICATION DATA
THOMAS, KATRIN. YOU'RE THE TOP: A LOVE SONG BY COLE PORTER/
INTRODUCTION BY BOBBY SHORT: EDITED BY PAMELA PRINCE AND
JANE HANDEL; PHOTOGRAPHY BY KATRIN THOMAS.
P. CM.
1. PORTER, COLE, 1891-1964. ANYTHING GOES. YOU'RE THE TOP.
2. POPULAR MUSIC—1931-1940—PICTORIAL WORKS. I. PRINCE, PAMELA.
II. HANDEL, JANE. III. TITLE
ML410.P7844T46 1999
782.42164'0268—DC21   98-37785 CIP   MN
ISBN 0-684-85560-7

SIMON & SCHUSTER EDITIONS